MW00974919

MICHAEL L. PRINTZ

and the Story of the
Michael L. Printz Award

GREAT ACHIEVEMENT
A·W·A·R·D·S

P.O. Box 196
Hockessin, Delaware 19707

GREAT ACHIEVEMENT
A · W · A · R · D · S

Titles in the Series

Visit us on the web at www.mitchelllane.com
Comments? Email us at mitchelllane@mitchelllane.com

TABLE OF CONTENTS

Printing   2   3   4   5   6   7   8   9
Library of Congress Cataloging-in-Publication Data
Bankston, John, 1974-
      Michael L. Printz and the story of the Michael L. Printz Award / John Bankston.
        p. cm. — (Great achievement awards)
      Summary: Profiles high school librarian Michael L. Printz, whose efforts in championing authors and their books led to the creation of the Michael L. Printz Award to honor excellence in Young Adult literature.
Includes bibliographical references and index.
      ISBN 1-58415-182-X (lib. bdg.)
      1. Printz, Mike—Juvenile literature. 2. High school librarians—United States—Biography—Juvenile literature. 3. Michael L. Printz Award—Juvenile literature. [1. Printz, Mike. 2. Librarians. 3. Michael L. Printz Award.] I. Title. II. Series.
      Z720.P74 B36 2003
      020'.90--dc21
                                               2002014333

ABOUT THE AUTHOR: Born in Boston, Massachusetts, John Bankston has written over three dozen biographies for young adults profiling scientists like Jonas Salk and Alexander Fleming, celebrities like Mandy Moore and Alicia Keys and great achievers like Coretta Scott King. An avid reader and writer, he has worked in Los Angeles, California as a producer, screenwriter and actor. Currently he is in pre-production on *Dancing at the Edge*, a semi-autobiographical film he hopes to film in Portland, Oregon. Last year he completed his first young adult novel, *18 to Look Younger*.

PHOTO CREDITS: Cover: Marilyn Miller; p. 6 Owen M. Henson; p. 10 Warner Bros.; p. 16 Bettmann/Corbis; p. 22 Jason Berryman; p. 25 Pam Spencer Holley; p. 28 Marilyn Miller; p. 32 Tim Keating; p. 34 Pam Spencer Holley; p. 35 Jason Berryman; p. 38 Michael Cart; p. 41 Jason Berryman; p. 42 Pam Spencer Holley

ACKNOWLEDGEMENTS: This story was written through the author's personal interviews with many people who were touched by Mike Printz in his lifetime. The author has every reason to believe in the truth and accuracy of his research. However, memory of past events may differ by individual. The author gratefully acknowledges the help of the following people in preparing this book: Michael Cart, Pam Spencer Holley, Marilyn Miller, Judy Druse, Dr. Owen Henson, Ken Underwood, Gene Floro, and Stan Seidel.

MICHAEL L. PRINTZ

Introduction
by Michael Cart

No one ever became famous for being a librarian. Why? Well, because in our media-driven culture people too often become famous for the wrong reasons. Personal integrity, a love of books, a passionate belief in their power to change young peoples' lives for the better, a deeply rooted respect for those same young people, and a lifelong commitment to serving them—none of these qualities and acts is likely to make someone's name a household word. But all of them distinguished my friend, the late Mike Printz who, for so many years, was the librarian at Topeka West High School in Topeka, Kansas.

Mike *was* famous among the countless students, librarians, teachers, authors, editors, and publishers whose lives were touched by his caring and by his stubborn commitment to excellence in library service and literature. But unfortunately, to the larger world, he was virtually unknown—like so many others whose life-changing achievements were centered on caring, on books and on service.

I was lucky enough to know Mike and to work with him in the Young Adult Library Services Association. Though we lived half-a-continent apart—he in Kansas and I in California—we kept in touch by telephone. And I was lucky enough to travel to Topeka often to visit him, to speak to his students, and to see him in action as a librarian of tremendous vision and innovation. In fact, the programs he created in Topeka became models for other librarians all over America.

When we, his friends in the Young Adult Library Services Association, recently created an important new award to honor the best books published each year for young adult readers, we instantly recognized it was an opportunity to honor Mike, as well. And so, unanimously, we named the prize The Michael L. Printz Award, knowing that this was the chance we had all hoped for to spread his name and fame and, moreover, to keep his name alive in such a wonderfully book-connected way.

Mike—like the authors who are and will be honored in the years to come by the prize that bears his name —was a great achiever. This long overdue biography offers compelling evidence of that.

And it gives you, the readers, a chance to meet a remarkable human being and to make his name a familiar word in the household of your hearts.

Michael Printz brought a sense of joy and wonder to nearly everything he did. His passion for books, and his compassion for his students, made him a great achiever even though he wasn't famous.

CHAPTER 1

AN "ORDINARY" MAN

T his book is a biography. A biography is a written history of someone's life—it is that person's story. Although a well-written biography can be as interesting as any fictional novel, the tale it tells is true. Authors of biographies try to be as accurate and stay as close to the facts as they possibly can.

Biographies are most commonly written about the famous.

The extraordinary lives of actors like Marilyn Monroe, authors like F. Scott Fitzgerald and sports stars like Michael Jordan have been captured in numerous biographies. Even the infamous are often the subjects of biographical profiles—criminals like Al Capone, dictators like Joseph Stalin, gunfighters like William "Billy the Kid" Bonney.

Probably few biographies are as popular as those about United States presidents— books on George Washington, Abraham Lincoln, John F. Kennedy and Franklin Delano Roosevelt could by themselves fill a small library. And recently, several biographies of presidents have been bestsellers, including ones about John Adams, Lyndon Baines Johnson and Harry Truman.

But not every biography is about a famous person. Biographies can be written about people who may not have been well known, but managed to do incredible things in their lives.

While books about people who live in mansions and drive sports cars might be interesting, there is often more to be learned by the tales of people who aren't millionaires, who aren't famous. They might labor in the shadows, but their work genuinely changes peoples' lives. Their efforts are not for fame, wealth or glory but because they genuinely care about other people and want to make a difference.

Ordinary people can be heroes. Any question of that was erased on September 11, 2001. On that date, anti-American terrorists piloted hijacked airplanes into the World Trade Center and the Pentagon. Over 3,000 people lost their lives. Among the dead were many people who tried to rescue them. More than 400 police and firefighters gave their lives trying to save others.

In the weeks and months that followed this incredible tragedy, people began to think about what it means to be a hero. Firefighters and police officers have been admired in the past. But in the late 20th century, fewer people gave them recognition for the risks of their jobs. Stories about police officers and firefighters during that time often focused on the negative—articles about the few who were corrupt or committed crimes. The many decent members of these professions were ignored.

But after September 11, 2001, people realized that the firefighters and police officers involved in the tragedy were heroes. Funds were set up to help the families they left behind. A postage stamp was issued in their honor.

And today, more than ever before, people realize that heroes don't have to live in Hollywood or run around on basketball courts or perform from rock music stages. Heroes can be next door. They're in our neighborhoods and in our schools.

This is the story of one such hero. His life and his death affected everyone he came in contact with.

Mike Printz was born, lived and died in Kansas. He was a high school librarian, a job that even other high school librarians describe as "not glamorous." Although his job might have been ordinary, what he did was extraordinary. By championing authors, he affected the words they wrote. By championing books, he expanded their audience.

For over three decades he influenced the lives of thousands of teenagers. He motivated the unsuccessful to succeed, the shy to be courageous, and challenged everyone he met to take the time and effort to question the way things are.

Mike Printz welcomed students who were below average in their studies. He didn't just call the kids who entered his library "scholars," he made them believe that they were. Yet at every opportunity he never failed to acknowledge the contributions that other people made. In one speech, he said that "all librarians have success stories, and those stories happen because of many people and not just one."

In 2000, his efforts began to be remembered by an award that was given in his name, in his honor. But before the award was created, there was his life. Michael Printz was one of the Great Achievers, and this is his biography.

Because most magazines, books, movies and television programs are produced in either New York or California, much of the rest of the country is ignored. Kansas is still best known as the setting for The Wizard of Oz. *Mike Printz didn't just teach students about the many inspirational people who called Kansas home, he convinced them that they could be one of them.*

KANSAS

To many kids, imagining Kansas is as easy as remembering *The Wizard of Oz*. That famous 1939 movie showed a desolate state beset by tornadoes and dust storms. Indeed, while the scenes showing Dorothy and her dog Toto's trek through Oz were photographed in luscious color, the opening and closing sequences in Kansas were filmed in grainy black and white!

Although Kansas in the 1930s was indeed a place filled with dying rural farms and storms of dirt, the state is much, much more than just a setting for *The Wizard of Oz*. It owns perhaps the most famous state song, "Home on the Range," which describes a place "where the buffalo roam and the deer and the antelope play." And while it's true there are more cows than people in Kansas—over two and a half of the animals for every man, woman and child in the state—that shouldn't be too surprising. After all, what do you expect from a place where every working farmer produces enough to feed more than 100 people? It is the number one producer of wheat and sorghum grain, and is also a top grower of corn and soybeans. Kansas is part of what is nicknamed "the nation's breadbasket." People who live there are proud of their state, as well they should be.

But while "Home on the Range" also describes a place "where seldom is heard a discouraging word," discouraging words about Kansas are common outside the state. The region Kansas is part of, the Midwest, rests in the center of the United States. But for many people it might as well be on the moon. Kids who grow up in the Midwest watch television and movies created in California; they read books and magazines published in New York. The vast expanse of our country between these two points is often insultingly described as "the flyover states."

Young adults growing up in states like Kansas get the message the media delivers: "The only way to succeed? Leave." And from 1990-1995, many of them did—according to population estimates the state lost over 10,000 residents, as more people moved away than moved in.

"Kids who grow up in the Midwest think that to make it big they've got to be on either coast," Michael Printz explained in an interview with *School Library Journal*.

But he didn't agree with that reasoning. "If you're willing to dream big enough, and work hard enough, you can do anything you want to right here in Topeka, Kansas," he said.

And Michael Larry Printz didn't just talk to other people about doing amazing things while living in Kansas—he actually did them himself.

The son of Floyd and Hazel Printz, Michael was born in Clay Center, Kansas on May 27, 1937. It was the height of the Depression, a period of time in our nation's history when the unemployment rate soared as high as 25%.

During World War I, much of the grassland in Kansas had been plowed over as food production increased drastically for the war effort. Then in the early 1930s, Mike's home state suffered through four rainless years. By the time he was born, farmers regularly endured "black blizzards," blinding storms of dirt which turned the region into part of a great Dust Bowl. Thousands who lived in Oklahoma, Kansas and other Midwestern states abandoned their homes and property for desperate moves to the west coast.

In Clay Center, jobs were hard to come by and money was tight. Fortunately, Michael's father had a good job at a local manufacturing firm.

Because of his work, Floyd was often gone. When he was home he was tired. Michael was an only child and the two spent very little time together. But for Michael, there was always his mother: Hazel. She was the one who encouraged his imagination, who convinced him he could do anything he set his mind to.

Michael was not yet five when the Japanese attack on Pearl Harbor sent the United States into World War II. The impact was immediate. The country, not yet recovered from the Depression, geared up for war. Jobs building airplanes, tanks, and other weapons became plentiful, but there were few things left to buy with these new wages. The steel once used for building cars now went into tanks and airplanes. The nylon that had been used to manufacture women's stockings became parachutes instead. Everything was rationed. Rationing is when restrictions are placed on available goods. It means you can't buy as much as you want to, even if you have the money.

But the Printzes were frugal. Hazel made sure she had enough gas saved up so she could take young Michael on Saturday drives. On long backcountry roads, the mother and her son embarked on their little adventures. These adventures fueled Michael's imagination and allowed him to picture life away from Clay Center.

Michael needed his imagination. In Clay Center, like most small towns, there wasn't much to do. For young people there was work on the farms, there was school, and there was whatever excitement they could create in their free time. Michael's free time was filled with books. Within their pages he could discover distant worlds, places he hadn't seen, events which had taken place long before he was even born.

Kids who read all the time often become writers. But Michael didn't want to be a writer. He wanted to share the joy he'd discovered in books with others.

In 1955, Mike graduated from Clay Center Community High School. After a year at the University of Kansas, he enrolled at Washburn University in Topeka. One hundred miles east and a world away from Clay Center, Topeka was definitely "the big city" to a young man who'd spent his life in small farming communities. It is the state's capitol and at the time that Mike was there, it boasted a population of over 100,000. That was a huge number for a small-town boy like Mike who'd grown up in a community with only a few thousand people.

Mike Printz thrived. He majored in English and history. And he imagined that he would become a teacher.

After graduating in 1960 with a bachelor of arts degree, he looked for a job. As is the case with many teachers, Michael's first position was at a small school. In fact he didn't get one job—he got two. Half of the time he was the librarian for tiny Onaga High School, which was about 50 miles northwest of Topeka. The other half he was an English teacher.

All teachers start off nervous and unsure, no matter what their training. But if Michael Printz was uncomfortable in a classroom his students didn't know it.

"He was just a young kid, I mean he wasn't much older than I was," recalls Ken Underwood, one of Mike's first students. "I can see him like it was yesterday. He was in control of the class." As Underwood remembered, "He was a great guy—he was almost one of us in a way. It's not easy coming in to teach a bunch of farm kids English and literature."

Michael wasn't just a good teacher—he was exceptional. The adjective might be overused, but what other word can you use to describe someone who is still fondly remembered by his students four decades later? Although Michael didn't continue as an English teacher, his lessons were not forgotten.

Ken Underwood was a gifted student at a time when there were few opportunities for such talents. He was rarely challenged by materials geared towards the middle student. Slower students were left behind and faster students grew bored. Ken would move his desk out to the school balcony, reading and ignoring the rest of the world. No one knew how to reach him.

Except for Michael Printz.

"He seemed to be most effective with the two extremes," fellow librarian Diane Goheen later explained to a reporter, "the really bright and the underdogs."

In a way, Ken Underwood was a bit of both. So Michael got the young man involved in drama, casting him in several plays. He taught Ken—and many other students—to appreciate books, to write effective, interesting sentences, and most importantly, how to think on their own.

"If we cannot teach young people how to work independently," Michael would later say, "we are in danger of becoming a nation of helpless people."

Today, Ken Underwood has earned a teaching credential, a new challenge for a man well into his fifties. Becoming a teacher might not have been a consideration if Michael Printz hadn't spent a year of his life as a part-time English teacher.

But despite Michael's skills in the classroom, it was in the library where he excelled. In the library, his love for books was given an audience, provided by the dozens of kids who entered the room every day. By the end of the school year, Michael knew what he wanted to do with the rest of his life.

Michael Printz would become a librarian.

But first the teacher needed to learn.

Thurgood Marshall was a talented lawyer who successfully argued the case of a young African-American girl who wanted to go to a nearby all-white school. Brown vs. Board of Education of Topeka was instrumental in desegregating schools and helped Marshall become the first African-American member of the Supreme Court.

TEACHING THE TEACHER

When Mike Printz decided to become a librarian he left the tiny school where he'd been working and headed for Emporia State. Located some seventy miles southwest of Topeka, Emporia State is a teacher's college, a place which trained the future educators of Kansas. It had also earned an outstanding reputation as a great place for budding librarians to learn. When Michael began his training he'd only spent two years as a teacher and part-time librarian, and that was at a school of just a few hundred students. But he knew he was ready.

Marilyn Miller was a big part of Michael's education. A full-time librarian, she was employed by one of the larger schools in Topeka. During the summer she taught a course at Emporia. It was Marilyn Miller's first year teaching library science and she was nervous. She wasn't too much older than her students, and too worried about making mistakes to really notice any of them.

"The first course I taught for the then-Emporia State Teachers College was in children's literature," she later recalled, "and I was so numb with what I didn't know that I am afraid I only remember one face from that course and it is not Mike's."

She might not have noticed him, but he sure noticed her.

She quickly became a mentor for Mike. In a speech, he later explained what Marilyn expected from her future librarians: "We must adapt to the new technologies; we must insist that service to students and teachers come before everything else, even filing cards in the card catalog. We must care about those young adults who attend our school."

That lesson wasn't difficult for Michael to take to heart.

"I remember thinking that I wanted to change thousands of lives," he recalled in his speech.

It was an emotion shared by many young people in the 1960s. In the southeastern Asian country of Vietnam, a war was raging—one which would eventually claim over 50,000 American lives. And in the United States, the election of the youthful President John F. Kennedy challenged the idealism of many young people like Mike Printz. The president's assassination in 1963 was a hard blow for them to deal with.

"Mike was deeply affected by the presidential efforts of Kennedy and his exhortations to service that he delivered so well to the American people," explained Miller. "Kennedy's death was a shattering experience for Mike."

After the assassination, she believes he became even more focused on what he considered important: service to others through librarianship, counseling and unselfish friendship.

Michael couldn't absorb the lessons fast enough. He knew that someone with access to knowledge could do more than just check out and catalog books. Becoming a librarian wasn't just about the Dewey Decimal System to Michael. It was about making a difference.

In 1964, Michael received his masters degree in library science from Emporia State. He was in that joyous position of knowing exactly what he wanted to do with his life.

In later years, Mike would return to both institutions—Washburn and Emporia State—to give back some of what they had provided him with. He taught a popular "Literature for Young Adults" class at Washburn and frequently came back to Emporia State in his capacity as a visiting professor in the Graduate School of Library and Information Management.

His first job after graduation was at Highland Park High School. Highland Park was smack in the middle of Topeka's African-American community. It was also smack in the middle of the enormous changes occurring across the country.

While the civil rights struggles faced by African-Americans in the southern United States are well known, many people forget that many of the battles for racial equality began in Kansas. Anti-slavery leader John Brown conducted his deadly raids on slavery supporters in the 1850s in Kansas territory. And a century later, another Brown would help change education in the United States.

Her name was Linda Brown. In 1951 she was an eight-year-old African-American girl who lived in Topeka, Kansas. All she wanted was to go to the elementary school a few blocks from her house. But that school was reserved for white students. The result was that in the 1950s, Linda and the other African-American students who lived near her had to walk two miles over busy downtown streets to reach the school that had been designated for them.

When her father and other parents sued the city's Board of Education, a lawyer named Thurgood Marshall argued their case. The case became famous as Brown vs. Board of Education of Topeka. In 1954, The United States Supreme Court ruled that separate educational facilities such as those in Topeka were illegal. It was the first step toward desegregating the nation's schools. It was a long, difficult process which began in Kansas. The case also helped to elevate Thurgood Marshall to become the first African-American member of the Supreme Court.

"Mike was one of those people who just loved working with kids," explained Judy Druse, who took a library sciences course from Printz in the late sixties, "and it didn't make any difference what color their skin was or whether they were immigrants or they'd lived here all their lives or whether they were lower socioeconomic or upper socioeconomic. He just had a real talent for reaching all kids."

The biggest problem Michael faced wasn't his students' poverty; it was the school's poverty. Public schools get most of their money from property taxes. These are based on the value of land, buildings and houses in the school district. Poor school districts usually have less money than rich ones. And often, sadly, the library is the last place to see any money.

Gene Floro knew Michael for over 30 years, beginning when the two met in their apartment building after Michael got his first full time library job. He remembers Michael as a man who didn't let financial obstacles get in his way.

"Because of his personality, and the fact that people related to him and really did like him, he could borrow what he needed. There were never huge funds to do things," Floro said.

Instead Michael made do at the Highland Park School. He scoured thrift stores, buying used furniture for his library so the students would have comfortable reading areas.

But there was one thing he didn't have: an office for himself.

Mary Chelton, an assistant professor at Emporia State, once asked him why there was no librarian's office.

"He said that he felt the librarian should be on the floor or in classrooms helping kids, and that the secretaries needed offices, so *they* had them, not him," she explained.

Michael could always make do with less. He quickly became adept at finding money for the projects he envisioned. And sometimes, for projects he hadn't even considered.

To Michael, libraries were about books. However, the 1960s brought as many changes to libraries as they did to the world outside of them. Technology was entering the building: reel-to-reel tape players, motion picture projectors, film strips. It was the universe of A/V—the audio-visual, multi-media center. And young Michael Printz was about to set the standards for their use.

In 1964, Marilyn Miller approached Michael about setting up his library to demonstrate the multi-media approach to gathering information. Although Michael was always more comfortable with books than technology, Miller remembered his response as, "OK. What do I have to do?"

With the help of colleagues, Mike took a library table, partitioned it into sections and set up a tape recorder, filmstrip projector, slide carousel and other pieces of equipment. As soon as all the different pieces of equipment were working he brought in teachers and students and demonstrated how they could use them for research, class projects and other assignments. Once again if Mike Printz was nervous, no one realized it.

Because of his work with the new multi-media setup, the federal government singled out his library for an impressive federal grant. And it wasn't just government officials who were noticing Mike. A few years earlier, Miller had left her librarian position at Topeka High School. She wanted Mike to be her replacement. The school was well funded. It would have offered the young man both tremendous opportunity and tremendous responsibility.

There was only one problem. He didn't want the job. "I will not follow you," he told her.

Michael wanted to carve out his own path. He turned down Marilyn's offer, a decision some might have considered foolish. But if that particular window of opportunity was sliding shut, a doorway was already opening up.

It was just around the corner.

Michael Printz, along with principal Dr. Owen Henson, set out to make the library at Topeka West High School an inviting place for learning and exploration. As this recent photo illustrates, they succeeded.

CHAPTER 4

GHOST TOWNS AND EX-PRESIDENTS

T he Topeka West High School was structured like a small college campus, with separate buildings for classes, adminis- tration, and—best of all—a well-stocked new library. When he was appointed to take it over in 1969, it would be all his.

Well, not quite.

"I made him the head librarian," former Topeka West Principal Dr. Owen Henson recalled, "and the person I had before him I made the assistant librarian. And she was a nice person, but she didn't have any vision about what a library ought to be. But he did."

Michael encountered an old-fashioned librarian in a new-fash- ioned library. But he refused to let the situation get to him. He worked with her as she approached retirement, even doing his least favorite task, cataloging. And he started proving how different he was from the stereotypical overly organized librarian.

Whenever new books arrived at the library, he'd give a "book talk," inviting small groups of students into the library. He'd discuss what each book was about with them. And then the kids would have a chance to check it out. If Michael hadn't cataloged it or even noted its call number, it didn't matter. He'd still let them take the book.

"If you could carry it, you could check it out of his library," Dr. Henson remembered with a chuckle. Once he even allowed a student to check out a plant! The young man needed it for his mother's remarriage.

Mike also worked to connect his students to the larger world. It might have started with the resources provided by a multi-media center, but it soon expanded to a program he developed with Dr. Henson: the Interim Adventure. In many ways it was a chance for some students to see their own future, while others got a look at worlds they barely knew existed. Some traveled all the way to San Diego to visit the U.S. Marine Corps base there, while others spent a day at a local hospital trailing a doctor. Dr. Henson's nephew went to a federal housing project in St. Louis, while other kids went north to the theaters of Minneapolis.

The program's popularity was immediate. By the time Mike and Dr. Henson arrived to register students for it at 6:00 a.m., the kids were already lined up. Some had spent the night on campus. There were limited spots for the activities and it was first-come, first-served.

"You think kids aren't eager to learn. Well, they are," said Dr. Henson, "if you design something exciting for them."

As the 200th anniversary of the signing of the Declaration of Independence approached, Mike began thinking about potential programs that would help mark the significance of the event.

"During the Bicentennial of the nation, I became concerned as to what students would remember about 1976 ten years hence," Mike later explained in a speech. "The commercialism bothered me."

Everywhere he looked, Mike saw tacky displays about our nation's founding fathers such as George and Martha Washington soap bars. These offered little or no insight into our country's history. He decided to change things. In that process, he began the program that earned him a national reputation.

"I decided to implement an oral history program at Topeka West," he explained in an interview. "Seniors enroll during their last semester. They are paired with a partner and assigned a significant

Being part of the Econo-Clad advisory committee gave Michael Printz a powerful voice in the world of young adult publishing. From left to right: Lucy Mark, Michael Cart, Susanna Swade, Mike Printz, Carlos Najera and Joy Lowe

event in Kansas history or a famous Kansan. During the next three months they prepare a thirty-minute video documentary concerning their topic. They raise all their own money, conduct interviews and after spending the last month of school sharing their findings with civic groups and school classes, they present their projects to the Kansas State Historical Society for scholars and researchers to use in the future."

He added that "I think it's great for kids to realize that something they did in 1983 or 1984 might be used fifty or sixty years from now. I think that gives a sense of their place in history."

So did their public presentations. What Mike called "Opening Night" would often be attended by up to 1,500 people. These weren't bored high school students who were forced to come. They were parents, friends, members of the community and respected civic leaders who were truly interested in the subjects being presented.

Dr. Henson remembers how careful Michael was with the students.

"Wherever those kids were, they had to call him every night," he said.

The students traveled to New York, to Los Angeles, and everywhere in between. If students encountered problems in these far-off locations, Mike would call on his nationwide network of friends to help out. As Dr. Henson remembered both in his years as principal and later as a superintendent, there were never any problems. All because of Mike Printz.

Once, a worried parent called Dr. Henson about her son. "My seventeen-year-old son is a senior at Topeka West and Mr. Printz wants him to go to New York," she complained.

Dr. Henson responded, "In another year he'll be eighteen and he can go to war."

She let her son go. So did most of the parents, as the program's popularity eclipsed even the Interim Adventure Program—one senior stayed in town after his family had moved to Louisiana just so he could participate. In 1991, a participant in the program traveled with Mike to the White House where she performed her one-woman show portraying three different women who had affected the life of President Dwight Eisenhower. The former president was a native Kansan.

Kansas also produced senator, presidential candidate and commercial spokesman Bob Dole, silent comedian Buster Keaton, Old West figures "Buffalo Bill" Cody and "Wild Bill Hickok," pioneer female airplane pilot Amelia Earhart, automaker Walter P. Chrysler, painter and sculptor Frederic Remington and scientist George Washington Carver. The landlocked state even produced Dr. Robert Ballard, the famed ocean explorer who discovered the sunken luxury liner *Titanic*.

Students who studied the accomplishments of such famous people learned one of Mike's greatest lessons: "One can hail from Kansas or any state and do anything they want with their lives."

In its sixteenth year, the Oral History program focused on a single topic: ghost towns. Mike got the idea from the book, *Ghost Towns of Kansas*. The seniors all studied the nearly deserted towns of Wilsley, Bushong, Iowa Point and White Cloud, interviewing former residents, examining historical records and visiting the regions. They were aided in their quest by the book's author, Dan Fitzgerald.

By then, introducing authors to his students was just one more way that Mike rewrote the book about being a high school librarian.

Most people wouldn't imagine that a high school student in Kansas would get the chance to meet well-known authors or travel the country. Yet if that student attended Topeka West, chances are that's exactly what happened.

CHAPTER 5

THE BOOK LOVER

Mike Printz loved books. He loved those who wrote them even more. When Mike began his career, books available for young adults—especially boys—were few and far between. Girls had some choices, but Henry Gregor Felsen's *Hot Rod* (written in 1949) and *Street Rod* (1953) were among the few that had much interest for boys.

He was especially impressed with Felsen's 1952 novel *Two and the Town*. Mike noted in an interview that it was "one of the first stories that ever dealt with a high school couple who had to get married. Felsen maybe paved the way for young adult literature with that."

In many ways the time in which Mike was a librarian was an amazing period for young adult books. S.E. Hinton's *The Outsiders* and numerous books by Judy Blume changed the way books for teens and pre-teens were written. Before there had been books for kids and books for adults, but suddenly in the 1970s that expanse between child and adult was being filled with literature.

And Mike was a huge part of that.

His love for books was a personal thing and so was his love for authors. How else to explain the shy way he pocketed the cigarette butt from smoking author Loula Grace Erdman? The Kansan who wrote *Many A Voyage* was the first writer Mike met, in 1960.

Over twenty years later, he was able to "provide young adults with the excitement of working with authors," as he described it. Once again a program Mike designed would have an enormous impact not just on his students' lives and on his own life, but also on the lives of authors as well.

By the 1980s, Mike had become very active in organizations that recommended books for libraries and helped in their promotion. His work with the Young Adult Library Services Association (YALSA) and distributor Econo-Clad meant that Mike had a perfect view of the numerous young adult books that appeared on the publishing landscape each year. Longtime friend Gene Floro remembers that Mike's apartment was stacked with books for the librarian to read. While Mike offered the insights of a longtime reader and someone who worked closely with teenagers, he did much, much more.

For one thing, he didn't just champion books written for young adults. He championed all books young adults would love. As a member of YALSA's Best Books Committee, he worked hard to get books that he believed in—such as *I Never Promised You a Rose Garden*—added to the organization's recommended reading list.

"I think we sometimes forget the mature, sensitive young adult who can handle adult books and adult interests," Mike admitted in an interview.

Besides just reading books for young adults, he got involved in their reviews as well. Every semester Mike enrolled half a dozen kids in an independent study course. He'd give them Best Books guidelines and the list of nominated books, then wait for their comments. Mike brought their reviews into the committee meetings and for the first time teenagers had a clear voice in the selection of the books. Before that, the Best Books list for young adults had been determined entirely by adults!

"He would gather a group of kids around him and have them review books for him," recalled Dr. Henson. "And whatever they wrote he stuck with them, you know even if it was a bit controversial. He valued their opinions."

Controversy and books are a combination as American as apple pie and ice cream. School libraries have censored, or banned, books by authors ranging from Mark Twain to Judy Blume. Mike hated censorship.

As part of an English class, a teacher showed a film based on Shirley Jackson's short story "The Lottery." The father of a student objected and demanded a hearing. He also asked to bring his minister. Dr. Henson agreed, but added he'd bring his own minister. He contacted the priest and then he spoke to Mike.

"He said, 'You know, you ought to have a student there,' Dr. Henson recalled. "And I thought, 'Man, I don't know whether I want to do that or not.' But he was so powerful with me, I did. And he never told me but I bet he had that kid research the biblical background of "The Lottery" and when I had that hearing, that young high school girl knew more than any of the rest of us in the room. Including both ministers. She blew 'em away. And the father just went out of there shaking his head and disappeared."

It was just one example of the way Mike Printz empowered his students to question, to think independently and to challenge the status quo, or the way things are. As much as he did that when the students were reading books, he got them to do it even more when they met the men and women who wrote them.

Gary Paulsen was one of Michael Printz's favorite authors. The books he wrote often appealed to boys who usually didn't read. Michael didn't just interest his students in Paulsen's books, he brought the author to Topeka West.

AUTHOR, AUTHOR

As impressive as his other programs were, his Authors in Residence program may be his greatest legacy. For by allowing authors a chance to work with the students who read their works, Mike influenced the way future books were written.

"Librarians have helped me to understand young people," author Gary Paulsen wrote in *A Printz of a Man*, a book about Mike. "It is fundamentally vital that a writer of books for young adults understand them, how they think, how they want to think and how they know things. Without this knowledge it becomes impossible, ridiculous, to write for them."

Of all the hundreds of school librarians Paulsen encountered in his career, Mike stood out. From the first time Paulsen met him, when the author was exhausted from just completing the Iditarod (a grueling sled dog race in Alaska) and nervous about an upcoming conference, he realized Mike "truly loved books. Loved the paper, loved the ink, the covers, even the process and that love in some wonderful way extended to the authors." The two became friends, and the writer contacted the librarian with problems, concerns, and even sent unpublished writing to Mike.

"I came to dedicate a book to Mike, *The Island*, and when I called to tell him he hesitated and choked up a bit and said that he was truly honored and wasn't sure he deserved it," Paulsen added.

Michael Printz taught his students that despite being from Kansas, they could accomplish anything they wanted to. Here he is (left) with (left to right) Pam Spencer Holley, successful Kansan, former Senator Bob Dole, and student Shannon Murphy.

There was more to it than that of course. By the early 1980s, Mike Printz had become a real power in young adult publishing. "Because of Mike's position with review committees and boards and his eventual reputation," Floro explained, "he was able to help authors succeed. Mike had a strong 'behind the scenes' voice about which books would be chosen by libraries across the country. He even helped to determine which books would reach publishers."

Rocky Sickmann, who grew up in neighboring Missouri, had been a 22-year-old Marine guard at the U.S. Embassy in Tehran, Iran when Islamic militants captured it in November, 1979. They held Sickmann and 51 other hostages captive for nearly a year and a half. Soon after the hostages were released, Mike brought Rocky to Topeka West during a special week-long program that examined the Iranian hostage situation.

"He had gotten paper and pencil and while he was a hostage he'd kept a diary," Judy Druse remembered. "He was able to get it out with him and Mike was influential in helping the young man publish his account."

The book, entitled *Iranian Hostage: A Personal Diary*, was published by Topeka's Crawford Press in 1982.

Druse continued, "To me that's one of the things that was so amazing about Mike, because I think most Kansas high school students wouldn't find or feel any connection to Iranian hostages... And yet Mike was able to bring that information to these Kansas high school students and help them see how it was a part of their lives."

There is nothing wrong with having power or influence when it is used for positive things. Mike used his to get multiple author copies

The Authors in Residence Program was one of Mike Printz's crowning achievements. The opportunity to speak and work with students during intensive workshops gave writers a chance to meet their audience and students a chance to discover a love for writing. Here a plaque at the Topeka West High School lists the authors who have participated in the program.

from Econo-Clad when writers showed up at his school, and he was able to use his connections as an incentive to get authors to travel to Topeka.

Mike's Authors in Residence program was a two-day intensive workshop involving the writer and thirty high school students. During much of the time no other adults were involved as the group wrote, discussed and critiqued.

Author Chris Crutcher recalls how his experience with Topeka's program was a first for him. At the age of 39, he had just published *Stotan!*, his first book, when Mike called in 1985. First Mike told Crutcher what a wonderful book he had written. Then he invited him to come to Topeka for the Authors in Residence program. Crutcher was understandably nervous, but noted how two students were responsible for taking care of his travel arrangements and accommodations after Mike had convinced him to participate.

"The workshop wasn't for students with the best academic records," Crutcher explained in *A Printz of a Man*, "but rather for the students that teachers thought would benefit from it for any reason."

Since then, Crutcher has done many events.

"But none of those presentations or workshops sticks out in my mind with the clarity of that first one," he said. "He (Mike) had total confidence in me. Far more confidence than I had in myself.

"Within an hour, this workshop took on a life of its own; all I had to do was fall into the excitement and passion these kids had for writing, and hang on."

Afterwards Crutcher met with Mike in his library. "Could you feel it?" Mike asked Crutcher. "Could you feel what you brought to these kids?"

Crutcher could.

But there was more.

"It wasn't what I brought to those kids," he said. "It was the totality of what Mike Printz had created. It was the soft, powerful pressure of his invisible hand that opened the possibility for that experience. And I realized I got more than I gave, because Mike gave more than he got.

But Mike Printz characteristically turned the credit back to his authors. As he later noted in a speech, "I know these authors have changed lives."

One such author was Hazel Rochman, whose book *Somehow Tenderness Survives* was an account of apartheid, the racial separation laws in South Africa which until the 1990s gave black South Africans far fewer rights than whites.

"The book created an awareness in our school when the library sponsored a week of nationally known anti-apartheid speakers in library forums, film festivals, student art and poetry exhibits based upon that book," Mike recalled proudly.

As a result, students made decisions not to support companies who continued to do business in South Africa. Many spoke out about their feelings and new-found awareness—all because of an experience that began in the school's library.

Many life-changing experiences began in the Topeka West library. However, by 1994, the librarian's life was about to change as well.

After retiring from teaching, Michael Printz began working full time at Econo-Clad bringing with him the years of knowledge he developed as a librarian. Seated, left to right: Dr. Marilyn Miller, Dr. Joy Lowe, Linda Sittig and Deborah Taylor. Standing, left to right: Dr. Ron Studdert, Randy Enos, Pam Spencer Holley, Joel Shoemaker, Michael Cart and Mike Printz.

CHAPTER 7

WORLD'S OLDEST SENIOR

M ike Printz had worked as a librarian for over 30 years. At Topeka West High School in Topeka, Kansas, he'd overseen more than 160 Oral History projects, welcomed numerous authors to his Authors in Residence Program and affected countless lives.

In 1993 he received the Grolier Foundation Award, awarded annually by the American Library Association "to a librarian who has made an unusual contribution to the stimulation and guidance of reading by children and young people."

It provided national recognition for the extraordinary job that Mike had done for so many years on the local level.

But by that point he was ready to retire.

January 14, 1994 was his last day as a librarian at Topeka West. As he told a reporter, "I'm the world's oldest high school senior. It's been my life, but I've always known I'd know when the time came and I know. School always starts the next day."

Even as he welcomed his last author in residence—fittingly, it was Gary Paulsen, one of his all-time favorites—even as he prepared for a full-time career with book distributor Econo-Clad, Mike had a secret.

"I think it was very difficult for him to retire," acknowledged his friend Gene Floro. "But he also felt that things were changing and it was time to get out of it and I believe his health was starting to fail."

Mike had a heart condition, and the last years of his job had taken their toll. Even after he retired he spent two more years working for Econo-Clad. He traveled across the country to seminars and conventions, recommending books to libraries and making a continued impact upon the world of young adult literature.

Unfortunately by the middle of 1996 he needed a heart bypass, a very serious operation. The day before the surgery, Gene learned from Mike's doctor that without it the former librarian only had a few months to live. Mike had kept that news to himself.

Dorothy Broderick, who edited *A Printz of a Man*, wrote that "September 28, 1996 was a very gray day in Kansas. As I stood in the backyard after dinner, trying to ease some of the tension that had built each day following Mike's operation on September 9, the clouds in the east magically disappeared and the full moon shone brightly. Then, gradually, a dark shadow crept across the moon, little by little blocking out the moon until the eclipse was complete. I could not help but think that Mike Printz was, for many of us, our full moon, and that little by little he was being removed from our lives."

The following day, Mike Printz died from complications following the surgery. He was 59.

The tributes to his life, and his work, began almost immediately.

"The ache I feel is my wish that he could have accepted for himself what he so readily gave to us, readers and writers alike," author Crutcher said. "A place to stand in the circle of joy and heartache that is story telling."

The Topeka *Capital-Journal* wrote on October 1, 1996, that "Mike Printz was a kind of travel agent for life. He took Topeka students through books and oral history projects, on wondrous journeys they might never have experienced without his enlightened guidance."

After his death, a plaque commemorating Michael Printz's life and work was placed at the library in Topeka West High School. The library was renamed the Mike Printz Library in his honor.

Gary Paulsen said simply, "I will miss Mike every day for the rest of my life."

Mike Printz was not a writer, but he stood within their circle, and for much of his life that place was inside the walls of the Topeka

From finding teenage reviewers for YALSA's best books list to helping book distributor Econo-Clad, Michael Printz made his love for books the focus of his life. Here he meets with the Econo-Clad Advisory Group at Econo-Clad Headquarters. Seated, left to right: Joy Lowe, Carlos Najera, Mike Printz, Pam Spencer Holley, Carol Fox. Standing, left to right: Barb Lynn Johnson, Michael Lunskis, Judy Druse.

West Library. On November 2, just over a month after Mike had died, his former principal Dr. Owen Henson unveiled a bas relief of the librarian's likeness during a special tribute ceremony at the place where Mike Printz had worked for over 22 years.

"In 1966, I visited a school—The College de Geneve in Geneva, Switzerland," Dr. Henson said at the ceremony. "It was built in 1558 and Napoleon addressed his troops from the balcony. Carved above the entrance were the Latin words, 'Post Tenebras Lux,'—'After the darkness, light.' After this darkness and because of Mike Printz, there will be a light."

That light shone brighter when the Topeka Board of Education voted unanimously to name the library at Topeka West after Mike

Printz. And soon afterward, the board of YALSA made a decision that will keep the librarian's light burning far into the future.

In January of 1999, the YALSA board approved the Michael L. Printz Award for Excellence in Young Adult Literature. As Michael Cart, who ran the task force for the award, noted, the idea of such an award actually started while Mike was still alive.

Lauren Adams, senior editor of *The Horn Book Magazine*, explained in an article entitled "The Year of the Printz" that "the award was created out of the belief that young adult literature has grown in scope and quality and deserves its own recognition, equivalent to that of the Newbery Medal for juvenile literature."

Cart originally kept Mike's name off of the award, hoping to generate a decision by as many members as possible. "I was explaining why we didn't have a recommendation for a name," Cart recalls, "and someone on the board said, 'Well then, why don't we call it the Mike Printz Award?' and everybody said, 'Yes!'"

The Michael L. Printz Award for Excellence in Literature for Young Adults was given out for the first time in 2000. The winner was Walter Dean Myer's novel *Monster*, about a 16-year-old who is arrested and charged with murder.

From now on, the award-winning book will be chosen each year from fiction, non-fiction, poetry—anything, so long as it's written for young adults. The creators of the award hope it carries on Mike's name, and the great work he did, for generations.

"Here's a local, high school librarian," remembered Dr. Henson, "who had impact all across the nation."

Mike Printz didn't just change libraries. He changed lives.

THE MICHAEL L. PRINTZ AWARD

Award Winners 2000-2003 (The award was first given in 2000)

2003 - Aidan Chambers, *Postcards from No Man's Land,* Dutton Books/Penguin Putnam Inc.

2002 - An Na, *A Step From Heaven*, Front Street

2001 - David Almond, *Kit's Wilderness*, Delacorte Press

2000 - Walter Dean Myers, *Monster*, HarperCollins

CHRONOLOGY

1937	born on May 27 in Clay Center, Kansas
1955	graduates from Clay Center Community High School; enrolls at the University of Kansas at Lawrence
1956	transfers to Washburn University
1960	receives Bachelor of Arts Degrees in English and History from Washburn University
1960	takes split position as half time teacher/librarian at Onaga High School
1962	becomes librarian at Highland Park High School
1964	receives Masters Degree in Library Science from Emporia State
1969	begins working as librarian at Topeka West High School
1976	institutes Oral History projects
1983	begins "Authors in Residence" Program
1988	named Teacher of the Year for Topeka Unified School District
1993	receives Grolier Award from American Library Association (ALA)
1994	retires from Topeka West High School; begins working full time as a marketing consultant at Econo-Clad Books
1996	dies on September 29, the result of complications during heart surgery; library at Topeka West is named in his honor
2000	Michael L. Printz Award is first given by the Young Adult Library Services Association (YALSA) of the American Library Association

EVENTS IN MICHAEL PRINTZ'S LIFETIME

1939	Nazi Germany invades Poland; England and France declare war to begin World War II
1941	Japanese sneak attack against Pearl Harbor prompts US to enter World War II
1945	World War II ends
1947	Jackie Robinson becomes first African-American to play major league baseball
1950	Korean War begins
1953	death of Soviet dictator Joseph Stalin
1954	Supreme Court decision in Brown vs. Board of Education of Topeka forces end of racial segregation in US schools
1957	Soviet Union launches Sputnik, the first artificial earth satellite
1960	Hawaii becomes 50th U.S. state
1963	President John F. Kennedy is assassinated
1964	Beatles make first U.S. appearance
1968	Martin Luther King is assassinated
1969	U.S. astronaut Neil Armstrong becomes first man to walk on the moon
1976	United States celebrates Bicentennial—the 200th anniversary of signing of the Declaration of Independence
1977	singer Elvis Presley dies of drug overdose
1981	Ronald Reagan inaugurated as 40th U.S. president
1986	Space Shuttle Challenger explodes shortly after liftoff, killing all aboard including teacher Christa McAuliffe
1989	Berlin Wall is demolished
1991	Persian Gulf War
1994	apartheid ends in Union of South Africa
1996	Olympic Games held in Atlanta, Georgia

FURTHER READING

While there are not any other books about Michael Printz, there are numerous works available about the state and the job he loved.

Kansas

Bjorklund, Ruth. *Kansas*. Tarrytown, NY: Benchmark Books, 2000.

Masters, Nancy Robinson. *America the Beautiful: Kansas*. New York: Grolier Publishing, 1999.

Libraries

Lermer, Fred. *Libraries Through the Ages*. New York: The Continuum Publishing Company, 1999.

Malam, John. *Library: From Ancient Scrolls to the World Wide Web*. Chicago: NTC/Contemporary Publishing Group, 2000.

Munro, Roxie and Julie Cummins. *The Inside—Outside Book of Libraries*. New York: Dutton Children's Books, 1996.

ON THE INTERNET:

To learn more about Mike Printz and the Michael L. Printz Award, go to http://www.ala.org/yalsa/printz

WORKS CONSULTED:

Broderick, Dorothy M., ed. *A Printz of a Man: A Festschrift in Honor of Mike Printz*. Chicago: Young Adult Library Services Association, 1997.

The author wishes to thank the following people who generously consented to an interview:

Pam Spencer Holly - May 1, 2002

Michael Cart - May 2, 2002

Marilyn Miller - July 25, 2002

Judy Druse - July 25, 2002

Dr. Owen Henson - July 30, 2002

Ken Underwood - August 1, 2002

Gene Floro - August 1, 2002

GLOSSARY

apartheid   (a-PAR-tight) the racial separation laws in South Africa which until the 1990s gave black South Africans far fewer rights than whites.

audiovisual   (aw-dee-oh-VIZH-yoo-wel) materials which involve sight and/or sound, such as tapes, CDs, DVDs or movies

barcode   (BAR-kohd) vertical lines which can be read by a computer, used on everything from books to groceries

bas relief   (BAH re-LEEF) form of sculpture in which the design is slightly raised from the background

cataloguing   (CAT-ihl-og-ing) organizing material in the library, usually using the Dewey Decimal System

Dewey Decimal System   (DEW-ee DES-mil SIS-tem) a numerical system used to group nonfiction books first used in libraries in 1876

microfiche   (MY-krow-FEESH) a sheet of transparent plastic which contains words and pictures, often newspapers and magazines

multimedia   (MUL-tee-MEE-dya) a way of providing information in a variety of forms including text, pictures and sound

rationing   (RASH-ning) limiting the distribution of food, manufactured goods and other items

volume   (Vahl-yoom) book

INDEX